Contents

Ladybird

Ladybird books are widely available, but in case of
difficulty may be ordered by post or telephone from:

Ladybird Books – Cash Sales Department
Littlegate Road Paignton Devon TQ3 3BE
Telephone 0803 554761

A catalogue record for this book is available
from the British Library

Published by Ladybird Books Ltd Loughborough Leicestershire UK
Ladybird Books Inc Auburn Maine 04210 USA

Two
Minute
Puppy
Tales

by Tony Bradman

illustrated by Kim Blundell

Now Here's a Young Puppy

Now here's a young puppy
Who looks very sweet,
With his long velvet ears
And over-sized feet;

With his little white teeth
And eyes deeply brown,
His tail always wagging,
A patch on his crown.

But he's full of mischief,
Of trouble and fun,
As these tales will tell you,
Once you have begun.

So you'll soon discover
What all puppies do;
They're nice, and they're naughty...
They sound just like you!

Turn over
for another
story.

5

The Puppy
Who Lost His Bark

Patch was a young puppy who couldn't stop barking.

It was the first thing he did when he woke up every morning, and the last thing he did every night. He went, "WOOF-WOOF-WOOF!" all day long. Sometimes he even barked in his sleep.

"Do you have to be so noisy, Patch?" his mum often said. Patch would simply go "WOOF!" and nod his head.

"I wish you were quieter, Patch," his dad would sigh.

"WOOF-WOOF-WOOF!" would be Patch's reply.

6

Then one fateful day, something
AMAZING happened. Patch woke up
in his basket, opened his mouth...
and nothing came out! His mum and dad
could hardly believe their big, floppy ears.

Patch had lost his bark!

He was as
surprised as they
were. He kept
opening his
mouth and trying
to bark, but he
couldn't raise a
single, tiny yap.
Patch was completely
and utterly... WOOF less.

To begin with, his mum and dad
were rather relieved. This was the first
peace and quiet they'd had since Patch
had been born. It was lovely living in a
WOOF-free house... or was it?

After a while they began to worry.

"Do you feel all right, Patch?" his mum
said.

Patch looked up at her and shook his head.

"There, there, Patch," said his dad.
"Don't cry."

A little whimper was Patch's only reply.

Patch felt hot, and his throat was sore,
and soon the doctor was at the door.
Patch had a temperature, he'd caught a
nasty bug. He had to have some medicine
and stay cuddled up snug.

The next morning, Patch was MUCH
better. He woke up in his basket, opened
his mouth… and went "YAP!" Then he
went, "YAP-YAP-YAP!" and followed that
with a… "WOOF-WOOF-WOOF!"

His mum and dad winced. They realised
they were probably in for a very noisy
day. But they looked at Patch and
thought, "Actually we wouldn't want to
have him… any other way!"

Another story tomorrow.

The Puppy
Who Wanted to Be a Cat

Life seemed far too busy for Penny the puppy. There was always something her parents wanted her to do, and she was fed up with it. So one day, Penny decided to be... a cat.

"Cats can do whatever they like," Penny said to her brother and sister. "I mean, just look at Ginger!"

Penny and her family shared the house with Ginger the cat. He did an awful lot of dozing, and was never, ever in a hurry.

"You're a dog," said Penny's brother. "You can't be a cat."

"Oh, can't I?" said Penny. "We'll soon see about that!"

From then on, Penny copied everything Ginger did. She walked like a cat, stretched out on the rug like a cat, and even tried to miaow like a cat, although that was quite hard.

And when her parents told her to do something, she said, "I'm sorry, I can't do that. I'm a cat!"

As you can imagine, after a while, this started to drive her parents CRAZY. So they came up with a plan...

The next morning Penny got a surprise. At breakfast, her brother's bowl was full of lovely, chunky dog food, and so was her sister's. But Penny's contained something rather strange.

"What's THIS?" said Penny, sniffing at it.

"Well, it seems you're a cat now," said her mother, "so we thought you ought to have... CAT FOOD for your meals."

Suddenly Penny wasn't sure being a cat was such a good idea.

How could Ginger eat this disgusting stuff? It was SO yucky...

The rest of the family burst out laughing at the look on Penny's face. Penny laughed too when her father took away the bowl with the cat food in it, and produced a proper breakfast.

And from then on Penny was a puppy again. At least she was – until she saw a bird flying through the sky…

"Don't be absurd," said her sister. "You can't be a bird!"

But Penny's parents wouldn't put anything past her…

And neither would I!

Another story tomorrow.

A Puppy Tail!

There's a puppy called Pippa
Who just loves to play,
She runs and she jumps
And she frolics all day;
She clambers and scampers,
And she never fails
To go running in circles
And chasing her tail.

Round like a whirlwind,
Round in a blur,
A small, dashing ball
Of teeth, paws and fur;
Round till she falls
And can chase it no more,
And lies pooped and panting,
Collapsed on the floor.

But Pippa's a puppy
Who just can't be beat;
Which means in a minute
She's back on her feet;
She KNOWS she can do it,
She's SURE she won't fail...
That's why she's a puppy
Who chases her tail!

Turn over for another puppy rhyme.

At Percy's Birthday Party

Percy the puppy is one today,
And he's having a party – hip hooray!
The doorbell's ringing, so let them in,
Now is the time for the fun to begin.

Come one, come all
And have a ball
At Percy's birthday party!

The table is laid with food galore,
And lots of it ends up thrown on the floor;
The cake is delicious, soft and sweet...
Just right for treading in with your feet!

Come one, come all...

Next Percy says,
"It's time for some games,
Like *Musical Chairs* and *Guessing the Names*,
And *Jumping to Catch a Floating Balloon*,
And *Forming a Queue to Howl at the Moon*."

Come one, come all...

Percy, alas, begins to play rough;
And Mum is soon saying,
   "Enough is enough!"
Percy's in danger of losing a friend...
Thank goodness his party
   has come to an end!

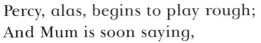

Come one, come all...

Percy the puppy
   has gone off to bed;
(Mum's sitting downstairs
   with an aching head);
He's had a great party – hip hooray!
It really has been a wonderful day!

Come one, come all
And have a ball
At Percy's birthday party!

Turn over
for another
puppy rhyme.

21

Five Little Puppies

Five little puppies
Having lots of fun,
Along came a little girl
And took Number One.

Four little puppies
Playing peek-a-boo,
Along came a little boy
And took Number Two.

Three little puppies
Racing round a tree,
Along came a little girl
And took Number Three.

Two little puppies
Rolling on the floor,
Along came a little boy,
And took Number Four.

One little puppy
Waiting on his own,
That's when I came along...
And took MY puppy home.

Another
story tomorrow.

23

Good Boy, Pickle!

Pickle the puppy was beginning to think he would never be able to do ANYTHING right. He tried his very best to be good, but whatever he did seemed to turn out wrong.

This morning, for instance, Pickle woke up in his basket, and set off to start the day in his favourite way... with something yummy to eat from his big bowl in the kitchen.

"Good boy, Pickle!" Tom said, and patted his head.

But he didn't say that when Pickle did some more eating a little later. Instead, Tom said, "Oh no, Pickle! You mustn't eat Dad's breakfast!"

Next, Tom and his family took Pickle for a long walk in the park. Pickle really enjoyed himself, and when he made a puddle by a big tree, everyone seemed to think it was wonderful.

"Good boy, Pickle!" Tom said, and patted his head.

But he didn't say that when Pickle made another puddle a little later. Instead, Tom said, "Oh no, Pickle! You mustn't do puddles there!"

At home, Pickle went to the corner where he kept the old bone Tom had given him. Pickle loved chewing, and after a few minutes of crunching and cracking he forgot his troubles.

"Good boy, Pickle!" Tom said, and patted his head.

But he didn't say that when Pickle did some more chewing a little later. Instead, Tom said, "Oh no, Pickle! You mustn't chew the table leg! You're a naughty, naughty puppy!"

Tom picked Pickle up and held him close to his face. Tom looked cross... but then Pickle suddenly thought of what he should do. He stuck out his tongue – and licked Tom's nose!

"Good boy, Pickle!" said Tom, giggling in between the slurps. "But you'll have to stop now. You're tickling, Pickle!"

But Pickle just kept on licking. He wasn't about to give up doing the only thing he seemed to have got right all day...

Another story tomorrow.

The Puppy
Who Went Exploring

Prudence the puppy was very excited. It had been such a thrilling day! She had started it living in one place, and now she was living somewhere completely different.

Her family had moved into a new house. Prudence couldn't wait to go exploring, even though she'd be going on her own. Her mum and dad and sisters all said they had too much to do.

"See you later, everybody," she said, and trotted off.

"Don't get into any mischief, now," her dad called out.

"Really," thought Prudence, "as if I would!"

Prudence went through the nearest door, and found herself approaching a cave full of interesting things. She snuffled inside it for a while, but then the things attacked her.

"Yikes!" said Prudence, "I'm off!"

She skidded into a nearby room, where she saw a strange box thing standing in the corner. She stood on her hind legs and sniffed at it… and suddenly it made a very loud noise!

"Yikes!" said Prudence, "I'm off!"

She scampered up the stairs and dashed into another room. There she found a big, puffy thing that was just right for biting and tugging at… but it tried to smother her!

"Yikes!" said Prudence, "I'm off!"

She shot across the landing, rolled down the stairs, and landed at the bottom with a BUMP! And that's where the rest of the family found her when they came running.

"Prudence!" said her mum. "What DO you think you're up to?"

"Quick, everybody," said Prudence breathlessly. "Let's get out of here before it's too late…"

When they'd stopped laughing, Prudence's family showed her round the house. She discovered the cave was a broom cupboard, the box thing was a television, and the puffy thing a duvet.

To make her feel more cheerful, her dad found her a bone. And next time she went exploring–she didn't go alone!

Another story tomorrow.

My Puppy Loves His Basket

My puppy loves his basket,
He loves his blanket, too,
He loves to eat his dinner,
He loves a shoe to chew;
He loves his tummy tickled,
He loves to play with toys,
He loves some rough and tumble,
He loves to make a noise;
He loves to go out walking,
He loves his favourite tree;
He also loves a person...
I'm glad to say it's ME!

Turn over for another puppy rhyme.

Polly

Polly was a puppy,
Small and trim and neat,
A puppy with a hobby...
Polly liked to eat.
Her tummy always rumbled,
It couldn't get enough;
Polly had to keep it filled
With lots of tasty stuff.

Beef and crunchy biscuits,
Sausages and lamb,
Chunks of red salami,
Mincemeat, rabbit, ham,
Fish and chips and bacon,
Chocolate bars and cheese,
Apple cores and marrowbones,
Dundee cake and peas.

Polly liked to root around
In dustbins for odd scraps,
And sit beneath the table
With her snout in people's laps,
Waiting for a present,
Or some food to simply fall;
It didn't matter how it came,
Polly ate it all.

Curry, tuna, muffins,
Cornflakes, cottage pie,
Ravioli, lettuce,
Wholemeal bread and rye,
Alphabet spaghetti,
Scrambled eggs and beans,
Sherbet dips and bagels,
Chicken legs and greens.

Polly kept on guzzling,
She ate and ate and ate,
And pretty soon she wasn't small,
Polly put on weight;
She grew in all directions,
An inch a day at least;
But did that stop her eating?
No! Her appetite INCREASED!

Liver, yoghourt, salad,
Burgers and French fries,
Jacket spuds and chilli,
Steak and kidney pies,
Doughnuts, Danish pastries,
Any kind of fish,
Apricots and jelly,
Quiches from the dish.

Polly WAS a puppy,
But now she's very big;
She uses loads of energy;
And still eats like a pig.
Her tummy's always rumbling,
Demanding tasty stuff;
It doesn't matter what she eats,
She'll never get enough!

Carrots, onions, cherries,
Samosas, Christmas cakes,
Cauliflower, rhubarb,
Mangoes, strawberry shakes,
Coffee, toffee, mustard,
Custard piping hot;
Whatever food that she can find...
Polly eats the lot!

Turn over for another puppy rhyme.

41

A Puppy Goes Walking

There once was a puppy
Who hung round the door,
Leaping and yapping
And scratching the floor;
I knew what he wanted
Though he couldn't talk;
My puppy was desperate...
To go for a walk!

It took just a second
To clip on his lead,
And then he set off
At astonishing speed;
He zig-zagged all over
The pavement as well,
His snout twitching wildly
At each brand new smell.

He stared in amazement
At cars roaring by,
And hated the wet stuff
That fell from the sky;
He started to shiver,
He slowed to a crawl...
And soon his small paws
Were not moving at all.

I picked up my puppy
And he licked my cheek;
I knew what he wanted
Though he couldn't speak;
Home, and some dinner,
And plenty of rest...
A walk is exciting,
But snoozing is best!

The
end.